# A Bright
# New Boise

## by Samuel D. Hunter

A SAMUEL FRENCH ACTING EDITION

# SAMUEL
# FRENCH

FOUNDED 1830

NEW YORK HOLLYWOOD LONDON TORONTO

SAMUELFRENCH.COM

**ISBN 978-0-573-60245-0**    Printed in U.S.A.    #28026

### MUSIC USE NOTE

### IMPORTANT BILLING AND CREDIT
### REQUIREMENTS

***A BRIGHT NEW BOISE*** was commissioned and first produced by Partial Comfort Productions at the Wild Project in New York City (Chad Beckim and Molly Pearson, co-artistic directors). The production was directed by Davis McCallum, with dramaturgy by John M. Baker, with set design by Jason Simms, lighting design by Raquel Davis, costume design by Whitney Locher, sound design by Ryan Rumery and M. Florian Staab, and video design by Rocco DiSanti. The cast was as follows:

**WILL** . . . . . . . . . . . . . . . . . . . . . . . . . . . . . . . . . . . . . . . . . . . . Andrew Garman

**PAULINE** . . . . . . . . . . . . . . . . . . . . . . . . . . . . . . . . . . . . . . . Danielle Slavik

**ALEX** . . . . . . . . . . . . . . . . . . . . . . . . . . . . . . . . . . . . . . . . . . . Matt Farabee

**ANNA** . . . . . . . . . . . . . . . . . . . . . . . . . . . . . . . . . . . . . . . Sarah Nina Hayon

**LEROY** . . . . . . . . . . . . . . . . . . . . . . . . . . . . . . . . . . John Patrick Dougherty

# CHARACTERS

**WILL** - Late thirties, male.

**PAULINE** - Late thirties to early forties, female.

**ANNA** - Late twenties to early thirties, female.

**LEROY** - Early to mid twenties, male.

**ALEX** - 17, male.

**TWO MALE VOICES ON HOBBY LOBBY TV**

# SETTING

Aside from the scenes in the parking lot, the entire play takes place in a windowless breakroom of a Hobby Lobby in Boise, Idaho. Stark, flourescent lighting, white walls. A few cheap chairs and tables are in the space, along with a telephone on the wall, an ethernet port, lockers, maybe a vending machine or mini-fridge, and a mounted television. Some non-ironic corporate slogans or work schedules adorning the walls wouldn't be out of order.

# AUTHOR'S NOTES

"Hobby Lobby TV" should be a recording two men sitting behind a desk, with a very dull background, either completely unadorned or with a very cheap looking "Hobby Lobby" sign behind them. It should always be at an extremely low, barely perceptible volume (except when indicated), and the dialogue should be as plain, boring, and non-descript as possible. No effort should be made to make it funny, ironic, meaningful, etc. It should only be slow, low-pitched, monotonous chatter about new items, sales and promotions, new store locations, etc.

Dialogue written in italics is emphatic, slow, and deliberate; dialogue in ALL CAPS is impulsive, quick, explosive. Dialogue written in BOTH is a combination of the two.

A "/" indicates an overlap in dialogue.

If desired, an intermission can be taken between scenes six and seven.

## Scene One.

*(**WILL** stands in a parking lot, at night. Sounds of a freeway can be heard: passing semis, car horns, car stereos, etc, as well as the buzzing glow of neon signs and fluorescent lights overhead.)*

*(He stands with his eyes closed, listening to the noise.)*

**WILL.** Now.

...

...

...

Now.

...

...

...

Now.

...

...

...

Now.

*(The noise continues.)*

## Scene Two.

*(The breakroom. **WILL** sits facing **PAULINE**, whose back is to the television. **PAULINE** wears a bright red vest with a nametag and holds a clipboard.)*

*(An extreme close-up of ear surgery plays on the television.)*

**PAULINE.** So then the black guy comes up to the Asian lady and the white lady, and he's like, "I don't really understand what all this talk about unions is gonna get us. All they wanna do is take our money and decide who were going to vote for." And then the Asian lady is like, shocked, and she says, "They choose who you vote for?" And then the white lady says, "That's not what America is all about." And then there's a graphic, or... Shit, what the hell is...? It's like a pie chart. Yeah, it's like—I don't know, something about unions. Do you know anything about unions?

**WILL.** They're not good.

**PAULINE.** Yeah, exactly. That's the gist of the pie chart, anyway, so you get it. Sorry you couldn't just watch it, the damn VCR's broken. Everything here is falling apart, including me. Heh, you know.

**WILL.** Oh. Yeah, heh.

**PAULINE.** So anyway, don't try to unionize.

**WILL.** Oh, no, of course not.

**PAULINE.** They shut down a Hobby Lobby in Kansas City when they tried to unionize, so don't try to unionize.

**WILL.** I really won't.

**PAULINE.** Too bad you couldn't see the video, it's actually— it has a funny segment, like a cartoon?

**WILL.** Oh, okay.

**PAULINE.** Yeah, it's actually a pretty great company when it comes down to it. And they know how to run a business, everything is hooked up to the corporate office. We can't even turn the air conditioning on without calling South Carolina. I mean—I know that sounds annoying, but it's actually really great. Really, it's just—a well-oiled machine.

**WILL.** Yeah, I'm really glad you had an open position—

**PAULINE.** *(holding* **WILL***'s resume)* Says here you worked for Albertson's up in Couer d'Alene?

**WILL.** Uh—yes.

**PAULINE.** Uh huh. And how was that?

**WILL.** Oh, it was—fine, I guess.

**PAULINE.** I used to be assistant manager at Fred Meyer, you know Fred Meyer?

**WILL.** Oh yeah, of course.

**PAULINE.** It's kind of like an Albertsons.

*(quick pause)*

**WILL.** Y—yes.

*(***PAULINE*** continues to look through his resume.)*

**PAULINE.** You from Couer d'Alene originally?

**WILL.** The area, yeah.

**PAULINE.** Beautiful up there.

**WILL.** Yes, it really is.

**PAULINE.** What brings you down to Boise?

**WILL.** I guess—change in scenery more than anything else.

**PAULINE.** Yeah? Well, Boise's a good town. You'll like it here, it's grown a lot over the past ten years.

**WILL.** Yes, it really / seems like—

**PAULINE.** When I was a kid, it was nothing like this. Where we're sitting right now used to be cow pastures. Nowadays, all the surrounding towns just spill right into one another. Friend of mine lives in Caldwell, tells me sometimes it takes him forty minutes to get to work. We have honest-to-god city traffic, you believe that?

**WILL.** Yeah, I haven't been here since I was a kid, it's much different—

**PAULINE.** *(looking at the resume)* Why'd you switch to part time in 2004?

*(pause)*

**WILL.** What's that?

**PAULINE.** At Albertson's. You switched to part time in 2004, how come?

**WILL.** Oh, I had a—sort of a second job.

**PAULINE.** What was it?

**WILL.** Uh—I was, it was sort of like, uh—bookkeeping?

**PAULINE.** Why isn't it on your resume?

**WILL.** Well, it wasn't really… It was very specific, it was for a church.

**PAULINE.** So?

**WILL.** Oh, you just… I don't know, sometimes people—they make assumptions about who you are based on—

**PAULINE.** Hell, we're not like that, believe me. The guy who founded the company is all, like, Christian. David Green, that's the guy's name. You should read the statement of purpose for the company, it's all like—

**WILL.** Plus, all my other experience is in retail, I thought that was more important.

**PAULINE.** Huh. Well, anyway, I can get you started as soon as you like. Tomorrow, even. Pays $7.25 an hour, I'll try to put you on full time in nine months if I can, until then you work thirty-eight hours a week. Holidays are time and a half, Sundays are time and a quarter. Possible seventy cent raise after nine months.

**WILL.** Perfect.

**PAULINE.** Alright then. I'll go get your W-2, do you have your social security card and driver's license on you? I can take you out on the floor and we can get going on your training. I'll set up an appointment for the drug test for tomorrow morning. You have any questions?

**WILL.** Yeah, just—is that always on the TV in here?

*(**PAULINE** turns around, sees the television.)*

**PAULINE.** Goddammit. Motherfucker. Goddammit.

*(**PAULINE** gets up and goes to the television, looking at it.)*

Goddammit. What is that, an ear? That's an ear, isn't it? Goddammit.

*(**PAULINE** picks up the phone and dials a few numbers.)*

*(on the phone)* Leroy, go up to the roof and—. Yeah, it's an ear or something. Yeah well fuck you too, Leroy. *(hangs up)*

Sorry about that. Goddammit.

**WILL.** Why is—?

**PAULINE.** It's the satellite dish, I don't know. Sometimes it gets all screwy, is it raining outside?

**WILL.** A little bit, yeah.

**PAULINE.** Figures. The company has it's own dedicated channel—nothing much, just info on products, new stores, stuff like that. Sometimes the signal gets crossed with these medical whatevers.

*(looking at the television)*

Goddamn, would you look at that? How do you think that feels? Jesus Christ.

*(**WILL** cringes. **PAULINE** notices.)*

Don't worry, you'll get used to it. You're not gonna vomit, are you? Interviewed a girl last month, she almost threw up. I didn't hire her.

**WILL.** I'm fine, it's fine.

*(**ALEX** enters, iPod buds in his ears. He doesn't look at either **PAULINE** or **WILL** and sits down on one of the chairs, facing away from them.)*

*(**WILL** stares at **ALEX**.)*

**PAULINE.** *(re: **ALEX**)* He's twelve. From some former Soviet republic, doesn't speak English so we can work him seventy hours a week.

**WILL.** What?

**PAULINE.** I'm shitting you. He's a high school kid. Worked here last summer too.

*(to* **ALEX***)*

Hey. Hey, Alex. SAY HI TO WILL. HE'S NEW.

*(no response, nearly screaming)*

ALEX FUCKING SAY HI TO WILL. MAKE HIM FEEL WELCOME.

*(***ALEX** *barely looks up, does a half-hearted wave toward* **WILL***.* **WILL** *smiles, waves back.)*

**PAULINE.** Good worker, actually. Real accurate register counts.

**P.A. ANNOUNCEMENT (ANNA).** Mandy, personal call on line two. Mandy, line two.

**PAULINE.** Fuckin' Mandy. *(re: social security card and driver's license)* Can I grab those to make a copy?

*(no response)*

Will?

**WILL.** Uh—yeah, here.

*(***WILL** *hands her his social security card and driver's license,* **PAULINE** *exits.* **WILL** *continues to stare at* **ALEX***. After a moment,* **ALEX** *feels someone looking at him.)*

*(He looks behind him, seeing* **WILL***.* **WILL** *smiles warmly at him.* **ALEX** *smiles back, then goes back to his iPod.)*

*(***ALEX** *still feels* **WILL** *staring at his back, he looks back at* **WILL** *again.)*

**WILL.** What're you listening to?

**ALEX.** *(taking off his headphones)* What?

**WILL.** Sorry, I—I'm just wondering, what're you listening to?

**ALEX.** Villa-Lobos.

*(pause)*

**WILL.** Is that—pop music?

**ALEX.** He's a composer who mixed traditional Brazilian music with European classical music.

**WILL.** Oh. Wow. That's impressive.

**ALEX.** Yeah, well, I'm glad you're impressed, that means a lot.

(**ALEX** *looks away, putting his headphones back in.* **WILL** *keeps looking at him. Finally,* **ALEX** *looks at him.*)

**WILL.** *(reaching out a hand)* I'm Will. I just got hired.

(**ALEX** *takes out his ear buds.*)

**ALEX.** Wait, you wanna like, talk? *(pause)* I'm Alex.

*(pause)*

**WILL.** What other kinds of music do you listen to?

**ALEX.** Lots. Mostly modern composition.

**WILL.** What does that mean?

**ALEX.** Like, composers. Who are modern.

*(pause)*

**WILL.** Are you a / musician?

**ALEX.** I'm gonna listen to my music now if that's okay.

(**ALEX** *smiles at him, putting his headphones back in. He turns on his iPod, scrolling through the music.*)

**WILL.** Alex?

(**ALEX** *takes off one earbud, annoyed.*)

**ALEX.** Yeah?

**WILL.** I'm your father. When you were born your name was William. You were named after me.

(**PAULINE** *re-enters.*)

**PAULINE.** Okay, so here we are. If you can get these done fast, I should be able to train you on one of the registers before we close. Should be quick, if you remember anything from Albertson's, you'll be able to pick it up pretty—

*(With a burst of static, the television flips back to Hobby Lobby TV.* **ALEX** *hurries out of the room.)*

**PAULINE.** Ah, there we go. These two guys, they never say their names on the air for some reason. Everybody has guesses of what their names are. I think they both sound like they're kinda high, so I call this one Woody and this one Harrelson. Get it?

*(pause)*

**WILL.** No, sorry, I don't.

## Scene Three.

*(Later that night, back in the breakroom. The room is dark except for the glow of the television, still tuned to Hobby Lobby TV.)*

*(ANNA enters, cautiously making her way into the room. She sits at a breakroom table and takes out a book and a plastic bag full of jerky. She opens the book and begins to munch on the jerky.)*

*(After a moment, WILL enters holding a laptop, turning on the lights. ANNA lets out a little scream and drops her book. WILL, startled, lets out a little yell as well.)*

WILL. OH—

ANNA. I'm sorry. I'm sorry.

*(ANNA desperately starts grabbing her things.)*

WILL. No, I'm sorry—

ANNA. I'm leaving, I'll leave. I'm sorry, I just—

*(quick pause)*

I know this looks weird, but I was just reading, I wasn't doing anything strange, I just…

*(pause)*

Are you—? Wait, who are you?

WILL. I'm new, I just got hired today—

ANNA. *(relief)* Oh…my God, I thought you were from corporate. Oh my God.

WILL. Corporate?

ANNA. They send—the company, sometimes they send people from corporate to check out the store at night, after closing. Like, a surprise inspection.

WILL. Oh.

ANNA. They have a video about this, you didn't watch the video?

WILL. The—it was the VCR, it wasn't working.

*(pause)*

**ANNA.** Just—don't tell Pauline you saw me here after closing, okay?

**WILL.** As long as you don't tell her you saw me.

**ANNA.** Right. Ha, ha.

*(pause)*

I'm sorry, so what are you—?

**WILL.** *(holding up the laptop)* I don't have internet where I'm
staying right now. I noticed the plug-in thing earlier.

*(pause)*

How about you?

*(**ANNA** holds up her book, smiles awkwardly.)*

**WILL.** You can't read at home?

**ANNA.** Not really.

*(pause)*

I usually stick around until ten or eleven.

*(**WILL** hooks up his computer to the Ethernet jack, **ANNA**
awkwardly goes back to reading.)*

*(After a moment, **WILL** goes to the television, about to
turn it off.)*

**ANNA.** Could you—?  Sorry, I sort of like to keep it on.

**WILL.** Oh—

**ANNA.** I'd just—rather you didn't turn it off. If that's okay.

*(pause)*

You know, I can read in my car, I can—

**WILL.** No, it's—you were here first. I can come back later, I
can—sorry, how did you get back in the building?

**ANNA.** Oh, I… It's silly. I just hide in the silk flower section
right before closing. No one seems to notice when I
don't leave with them, I don't know. How did you get
back in?

*(pause)*

**WILL.** Fabric section.

> *(Short pause. They both start laughing, awkwardly at first.)*

**ANNA.** Are you serious?

**WILL.** Yep.

**ANNA.** That's—that's just ridiculous, isn't it?

**WILL.** Yes, I guess it is.

**ANNA.** Pretty bold move on your first day.

**WILL.** I used to do it at the Albertson's I worked at all the time.

**ANNA.** And I thought I was the only wacko who did this.

> *(**ANNA** smiles, walking toward **WILL** and extending a hand.)*

**ANNA.** I'm Anna.

**WILL.** Will.

**ANNA.** Well hello, Will!

> *(a terrible attempt at a joke)*

"Will" you be sneaking in—.

> *(Neither of them laugh. **ANNA** looks away in shame for a moment, then recovers.)*

**ANNA.** If you don't mind, you know—we could both stay, I could read, and you could do your—work or whatever. Do you have a job online? That's so interesting. I'm talking too much, am I talking too much?

**WILL.** No, it's fine—it's not really a job. I mean, it doesn't pay anything. I have a...

> *(pause)*

**ANNA.** What?

**WILL.** It's just so stupid, I...it's like—a blog. It's stupid, and I'm a big dork.

**ANNA.** That's not stupid! What are you talking about? A blog, that's so—hip. What kind of blog is it?

**WILL.** *(hesitating)* Um. It's...

**ANNA.** What am I doing? Shut up, Anna.

**WILL.** No, it's—it's like a story. Like a long story, like—an online novel.

*(pause)*

**ANNA.** Holy crap, you write books?

**WILL.** Well—

**ANNA.** I love books! I read books all the time! You're actually a writer?!

**WILL.** I don't get paid or anything—

**ANNA.** So?! Holy crap!

*(pause)*

Sorry, I just—you're a writer, that's so neat.

**WILL.** Well not lately. It's been kind of rough going.

**ANNA.** Writer's block?

**WILL.** Something like that. Keep forcing myself to sit down and write, but—nothing comes.

**ANNA.** Like a process. Like an artistic process, I get that, yep.

*(pause)*

Well, I bet your book is great. A lot better than what I'm reading right here, I bet that much. What's your book about?

**WILL.** It's, uh—sort of like—Christian Literature?

**ANNA.** Oh yeah? That's great! I read that one book, what's it called—"The Purpose Driven Life." Yeah, that was good. Anyway, I'm a Christian, I've always believed in Jesus.

**WILL.** Yeah?

**ANNA.** Sure, what else is there to believe in?

*(**WILL** smiles. Pause.)*

**ANNA.** Well, I need to let you work. You sure you don't need me to leave? I can leave—

**WILL.** No, I'd… it's nice to have company, actually.

*(Pause.* **ANNA** *goes back to reading smiles at him, then laughs a little.)*

**ANNA.** I'm sorry. I still just can't believe... Both of us hiding in here—

**WILL.** It's really pretty funny.

**ANNA.** It's so cute, I...

*(pause)*

Okay. I read, you write.

**WILL.** *(smiling)* Deal.

*(***ANNA*** opens up her book, ***WILL*** opens his laptop.)*

## Scene Four.

*(Early the next morning, in the parking lot.* **WILL** *stands facing* **ALEX**.*)*

**WILL.** Hi. *(pause)* Thanks for meeting me. I think I rushed my introduction just a little bit, I didn't want to—scare you.

*(pause)*

Did you tell your parents about me?

**ALEX.** No.

**WILL.** Okay. *(pause)* I can't imagine what you're feeling right now, I can't imagine what you've thought about me all these years—

**ALEX.** I don't believe you.

*(Silence.* **WILL** *takes a step toward* **ALEX***, who backs away.)*

**WILL.** I can tell you that you were born on May 22nd, that's your birthday, right? You have foster parents, their names are John and Cindy McDonald.

**ALEX.** Any idiot with access to Google could figure out all that.

*(pause)*

**WILL.** You have a birthmark on your lower back, on the right side. When you were little you had blonde hair, but I guess it got darker as you grew up.

*(**WILL** pulls out his wallet, taking out a weathered photograph.)*

That's you. At two months. That's me, holding you.

*(**ALEX** looks at the photograph, then hands it back to him.)*

**ALEX.** Whatever, all babies look the same.

*(pause)*

**WILL.** Look, Alex, I don't know how to prove this to you—

**ALEX.** How did you find me?

**WILL.** I tracked down John and Cindy years ago. They didn't want me to have any contact with you, but every year they send me a letter. About you. Like a—status report, I guess.

**ALEX.** Do you know John and Cindy?

**WILL.** No, I mean—not really—

**ALEX.** Yeah well, they're assholes. If you are my father, then fuck you, because you gave me to assholes.

*(pause)*

When I was little I used to have fantasies about my real dad coming to get me. Like he was a prisoner of war, or an FBI guy or something. He didn't work at the Hobby Lobby, that's for sure. Do you at least drive a cool car or live in a big house?

**WILL.** It's a '94 Subaru. And right now, it's also my house.

**ALEX.** I'm gonna kill myself.

**WILL.** What?

**ALEX.** Nothing, it's just something I say. So if you're really my father—again, if—what do you want from me? You better not need a kidney or something.

**WILL.** No, I don't, I... I just want to get to know you.

**ALEX.** Okay, but why now?

*(pause)*

**WILL.** Look, Alex, things in my life have sort of been turned upside down, and I've had to reconsider a lot of the decisions I've made, the things I believe in... I just want to make a fresh start.

**ALEX.** Huh. Well, good for you.

*(pause)*

I have panic attacks. Sometimes more than once a week. Do you know what a panic attack is?

**WILL.** Yeah—

**ALEX.** No, you don't. You think that you might, but you don't. You probably think that it's just about me being stressed out, you think that I have a panic attack when I get a bad grade on a test or something. I get panic attacks over nothing. Absolutely nothing. I'll be at work, or at home, or at school, and suddenly I'll start shaking and I won't be able to breathe.

(pause)

School counselor says that it might be a chemical imbalance. Or, she says, it might have something to do with my past. I think it has something to do with my past, so if you're my father, it's probably your fault.

(pause)

**WILL.** Maybe just lunch / sometime?

**ALEX.** I want a blood test.

(pause)

**WILL.** Okay. I can—I'm not really sure where to go, but I can find out, I can make some calls—

**ALEX.** Valley Medical Clinic. It's in Meridian, on 17th Street. I have an appointment for six, you have an appointment for seven. We're going separately, and you're paying for it. It's not cheap.

(pause)

**WILL.** Okay.

**ALEX.** And you need to know that if it turns out that you're my biological father, that doesn't necessarily mean anything. It doesn't mean I have to talk with you or interact with you in any way.

(pause)

**WILL.** Did you know that your real name is William?

**ALEX.** My real name isn't William.

**WILL.** It was the name your mother gave you when you were born.

**ALEX.** Don't ever call me William. If you call me William, I'm gonna kill myself.

**WILL.** I won't. I'm sorry.

**ALEX.** And don't talk about my mom unless I tell you to.

(*pause*)

**WILL.** I listened to some Villa-Lobos last night. Downloaded some albums.

**ALEX.** You did?

**WILL.** Yeah. Backa—?

**ALEX.** Bachianas Brasileiras.

**WILL.** Yeah.

**ALEX.** What did you think?

**WILL.** It was really pretty.

(*pause*)

**ALEX.** "Pretty"?

**WILL.** Yeah, and—

**ALEX.** (*under his breath*) …I'm gonna kill myself…

**WILL.** Overwhelming.

(*Pause.* **ALEX** *looks at him.*)

**ALEX.** If I ask you to quit and move out of Boise, would you?

(**WILL** *doesn't answer, staring down at his shoes.*)

I gotta clock in.

(**ALEX** *exits.*)

## Scene Five.

*(Later that day. **LEROY** sits in the breakroom reading a newspaper, wearing a T-shirt that reads simply "FUCK" in large block letters. Hobby Lobby TV plays in the background. After a moment, **WILL** enters with some lunch in a Tupperware container. He notices **LEROY**'s shirt, and nods politely at him.)*

*(**WILL** goes to the microwave, puts in his lunch, and turns it on.)*

**LEROY.** It's a piece of shit.

**WILL.** *(turning)* What's that?

**LEROY.** The microwave. It barely works, I'd recommend cranking it up to high and leaving it in there for at least three times longer than normal.

**WILL.** Oh—okay, thanks.

*(**WILL** turns the microwave up.)*

**LEROY.** How's the first day?

**WILL.** Second, actually. Well, first full day. It's—fine. Slow.

**LEROY.** It's always like this. You'd think they were losing money, but the profit margin is pretty amazing.

**WILL.** What do you mean?

**LEROY.** Think about it. They're just selling all this raw material; fabric, paint, balsa wood, whatever. It's like the customers are paying money to do the manufacturing process themselves. You know those foam balls, the ones we sell for ninety-nine cents, the one the size of a baseball?

**WILL.** Yeah.

**LEROY.** Those things cost less than a penny to make.

**WILL.** Is that right?

**LEROY.** That's right.

**WILL.** Wow. Highway robbery.

**LEROY.** What?

**WILL.** Oh, I just—that's a big markup.

**LEROY.** You think it's dishonest?

**WILL.** Oh, I—I didn't mean that—

**LEROY.** You didn't?

**WILL.** No, I was just… It was just a joke.

(*pause*)

**LEROY.** I'm deliberately making you uncomfortable.

(*Awkward pause.* **WILL** *turns off the microwave and takes out his lunch. He sits at a table across the room from* **LEROY** *and begins to eat.*)

(**LEROY** *grabs his newspaper and sits down next to* **WILL.**)

**LEROY.** (*extending a hand*) Leroy.

**WILL.** Oh, it's—

**LEROY.** Will. I know.

**WILL.** How do you know my—?

(**LEROY** *points to his nametag.*)

**WILL.** Oh. Heh.

(*pointing to* **LEROY**'s *shirt*)

So do you—? You actually wear that to work?

**LEROY.** For as long as I can before Pauline sees me.

**WILL.** You don't get in trouble?

**LEROY.** I'm the only one in this store who knows anything about art supplies, so I can basically do whatever I want. I'm the only one that can answer actual questions.

**WILL.** Are you an artist?

**LEROY.** Getting my masters in Fine Arts at BSU.

**WILL.** What kind of art to you make?

(**LEROY** *points to his T-shirt.*)

**WILL.** I—don't understand—

**LEROY.** I also have one that says "cunt", one that says "you will eat your children", and one that has a color photograph of my penis on both sides.

**WILL.** Oh.

**LEROY.** I'm forcing people to confront words and images they normally avoid. Especially at a place like this.

**WILL.** You—you mean the Hobby Lobby?

**LEROY.** Exactly. It's about the interaction between the word and the kinds of people who shop here, deliberately making them uncomfortable. Soccer moms and grade school kids and little old ladies, they all have to confront the reality of the words before they get their arts and crafts supplies. You want a foam ball? FUCK. You want some acrylic paints? CUNT. You want some pipe cleaners? YOU WILL EAT YOUR CHILDREN. It's the only reason I work here, I could have got some boring job on campus just as easy. But where's the art in that?

*(pause)*

**WILL.** Well, I'm just gonna finish up my—

**LEROY.** You just move to town?

**WILL.** Um. Yes, actually.

**LEROY.** Where from?

**WILL.** Up north.

**LEROY.** Where up north?

**WILL.** Outside of Couer d'Alene.

**LEROY.** Where outside of Couer d'Alene?

**WILL.** Um. Small town.

**LEROY.** Beautiful up there.

**WILL.** Yes, it is, it's really—  Have you spent time up there?

**LEROY.** Little bit. Family trips, you know. Things like that. Kootenai county, right?

**WILL.** That's right.

**LEROY.** Rathdrum—that's around there, isn't it?

*(pause)*

**WILL.** Yeah, that's actually—well, I grew up in Rathdrum.

**LEROY.** Is that right? Pretty small town, right?

**WILL.** Pretty small.

**LEROY.** Must be hard to be in Boise after such a nice little quiet town like that, huh?

**WILL.** Boise's actually / very nice—

**LEROY.** What was the name of that church up in Rathdrum? The one that was in the papers a few months ago— Life Church, New Order—?

**WILL.** New Life Fellowship.

**LEROY.** Right, New Life. I kind of lost track of the story after a while—is your pastor in jail yet, or is he still awaiting trial?

*(pause)*

You see this? This is me deliberately making you uncomfortable. This is your "FUCK" T-shirt.

*(pause)*

**WILL.** Well, I figured this would happen.

**LEROY.** I actually think this is kind of cool, it's like I'm talking to a survivor of Jonestown or something.

**WILL.** Is there a reason that you're doing this?

**LEROY.** Alex is my little brother. Adopted brother, whatever.

*(pause)*

**WILL.** I know how this looks. And you're right to be defensive but—honestly, after what happened, I'm just trying to start again.

**LEROY.** You still believe in all that?

**WILL.** I still believe in God.

**LEROY.** What about the other stuff? All that crazy crap your pastor was preaching about, you still believe in all that?

*(pause)*

**WILL.** I don't know. *(pause)* I'm trying to leave all that behind.

*(pause)*

**LEROY.** Okay, look. I read through some of the articles last night. From what I can tell, you didn't have anything to do with that kid who died. And I get that you coming down here is just your ham-fisted attempt to put your life on a new track. But you're going about this in the creepiest way possible, confronting him at work like this.

**WILL.** I didn't know what else to do, I was worried your parents wouldn't allow me to see him—

**LEROY.** Yeah, well, John and Cindy drink enough nowadays that they probably wouldn't even care that you're here. But believe me, I care.

*(pause)*

Just stay away from him, okay? Don't fuck with him. Don't try to "convert" him or whatever.

**WILL.** I won't. I don't do that anymore.

*(**PAULINE** enters with a clipboard, **WILL** and **LEROY** stop. She senses the tension in the room.)*

**PAULINE.** What?

**LEROY.** Nothing.

**PAULINE.** You making enemies already, Leroy?

**LEROY.** No—

**PAULINE.** Well, you better not, because the last thing I want to deal with today is fucking conflict resolution and I—

*(noticing **LEROY**'s shirt)*

LEROY TAKE THAT FUCKING SHIRT OFF.

**LEROY.** I didn't bring another one.

**PAULINE.** I CARE?!

*(**LEROY** takes the shirt off, putting his Hobby Lobby vest on over his bare torso.)*

**PAULINE.** Get out there, you're ten minutes late.

**LEROY.** Fuck you.

**PAULINE.** FUCK YOU.

*(LEROY exits.)*

**PAULINE.** Fucking hell I wish I could fire that self-righteous little—

**LEROY.** *(offstage)* FUCK YOU.

**PAULINE.** *(screaming)* FUCK YOU!

*(to WILL)*

You didn't completely fill out your contact sheet.

**WILL.** What?

**PAULINE.** Emergency contact.

**WILL.** Oh. Um.

**PAULINE.** Anybody. Family, friend, girlfriend, whatever. Doesn't have to be local.

**WILL.** I don't really—…

**PAULINE.** No family?

**WILL.** Not that I can—...

*(pause)*

**PAULINE.** It's for corporate. Gotta put something. Make up a name, I guess.

**WILL.** Okay.

*(PAULINE exits. WILL fills out the form.)*

## Scene Six.

*(The next morning. **ALEX** sits at a breakroom table, reviewing a spool of record tape from a register. Two other spools sit in front of him.)*

*(Hobby Lobby TV plays on the television.)*

*(**WILL** enters, stopping when he sees **ALEX**. **ALEX** looks at him. Awkward silence.)*

**WILL.** What's this?

*(No response. **ALEX** continues looking through the receipt tape.)*

**WILL.** Sorry.

**P.A. ANNOUNCEMENT (PAULINE).** Mandy to frontlines please. Mandy, frontlines.

*(**WILL** goes to a locker, taking out his vest and putting it on. He is about to exit when:)*

**ALEX.** Error in my register countdown yesterday.

*(**WILL** turns around.)*

**WILL.** Oh. How much?

**ALEX.** A hundred and sixty seven dollars short.

**WILL.** Ouch.

**ALEX.** I've never been more than a dollar off.

*(pause)*

Pauline wants me to look at the receipt logs for the entire day to see if I can figure out where I made the mistake. I don't even know what I'm looking for.

*(pause)*

**WILL.** Do you want me to—?

*(pause)*

I've done this a hundred times, when I was working at Albertson's I was off all the time.

*(Pause.* **ALEX** *puts one of the receipt spools at the seat across from him.* **WILL** *moves to the table and sits down.* **WILL** *opens up the receipt tape and starts to read it at an extremely fast pace.)*

**ALEX.** Are you really reading it?

**WILL.** I told you, I've done it a hundred times. My count-downs were always terrible. Trick is to look for too many zeros on the cash tenders. You can skip all the credits and debits.

*(Silence as they examine the record tape.)*

**ALEX.** They called me this morning.

**WILL.** The blood test?

*(pause)*

Do you believe me now?

**ALEX.** It doesn't change anything.

**WILL.** Okay.

*(They continue to look.)*

**WILL.** Is there anything you'd like to know?

**ALEX.** Like what?

**WILL.** About me, about—why you were put up for adoption—

*(**ANNA** enters holding the book from before. She smiles at **WILL**, **WILL** smiles back. **ANNA** sits down at a table.)*

**ALEX.** John and Cindy said my real parents were neo-Nazis.

**WILL.** That's not... Um.

**ALEX.** Well, that's what they said. They said my parents were a couple of neo-Nazis. Are you a neo-Nazi?

*(**ANNA** looks up from her book.)*

**WILL.** No. A—

**ALEX.** Actually, the story about you has changed a few times. When I was little, they told me that you both died in a car accident. Then later, it was that you were neo-Nazis. Then, they said that you beat me.

**WILL.** (*reading the receipt tape*) Maybe we should talk about this somewhere else.

(**ALEX** *looks at* **ANNA.**)

**ALEX.** Hi, Anna.

**ANNA.** Um.

**ALEX.** This is my father. His name is—

(**ALEX** *looks at* **WILL**'s *nametag.*)

Will. He put me up for adoption when I was a baby, and according to my parents he's a child-beating neo-Nazi who's dead.

(**ANNA** *closes her book and exits quickly.*)

(*silence*)

**WILL.** Found it.

**ALEX.** What?

(**WILL** *shows him the receipt tape.*)

**WILL.** See? It's a cash tendered. You entered two hundred instead of twenty.

(*pause*)

**ALEX.** I've never made a mistake like that before.

(**ALEX** *takes the receipt tape from him, circling the mistake.*)

(*not looking at* **WILL**) Thank you.

(*Pause.* **ALEX** *puts down the receipt tape, staring at his hands.*)

Okay, I want you to start talking. You'll start talking, you'll tell me things about yourself but when you say something I don't want to hear or don't care about, I'm going to say stop, and you're going to stop, and then say something different.

(**ALEX** *reaches into his backpack and takes out a large notebook and a pen. He opens to a page about a quarter of the way through and starts writing.*)

WILL. What's—?

ALEX. Stop.

*(Pause. **ALEX** continues to write.)*

WILL. You were born in a hospital in Couer / d'Alene—

ALEX. Stop.

*(pause)*

WILL. Your mother and I / were—

ALEX. Stop. I said things about you. Go.

*(pause)*

WILL. I grew up in Rathdrum. My parents were from there, too. It's a little town, about six thousand people. There's a little grocery store that my grandfather started, and my father ran it after he died, but it closed when—

ALEX. Stop. Boring.

WILL. I'm thirty-nine years / old—

ALEX. Stop.

*(pause)*

WILL. I didn't have anything to do with you being put up for / adoption—

ALEX. Stop.

WILL. Your mother left me after you / were born and she—

ALEX. Stop stop STOP. If you don't stop I'm going to kill myself.

*(**ALEX**'s breathing speeds up a bit. Long pause.)*

WILL. Okay, I—...I'm allergic to tuna, but it's not a terrible allergy so I eat it sometimes.

*(**ALEX** begins to calm down.)*

WILL. I don't own any decent pants and I don't know why. I don't like movies.

ALEX. *(still concentrating on his writing)* Why?

WILL. Because they're too violent.

**ALEX.** There's violence in the world.

**WILL.** But we don't need to take pleasure in it.

**ALEX.** That's a stupid thing to say.

(**PAULINE** *appears in the doorway.*)

**PAULINE.** MANDY?! You guys seen Mandy?

**ALEX.** No.

**PAULINE.** Fuckin' Mandy.

(**PAULINE** *exits. Pause.*)

**WILL.** There are things I regret.

(**ALEX** *stops, looks up at him momentarily, then continues writing.*)

More than regret. There are things that tear into me. Things that that make me physically ill.

**ALEX.** Stop. I don't care how you feel.

(*pause*)

Why were you hiding in the fabric section at closing the other day?

(*pause*)

**WILL.** You saw me?

**ALEX.** Yes.

(*pause*)

**WILL.** I just—needed a quiet place to do some work.

**ALEX.** What work?

**WILL.** I'd really rather not—

**ALEX.** Tell me.

**WILL.** Alex—

**ALEX.** Tell me or I'm gonna kill myself.

**WILL.** Why do you say that? You don't really mean that, do you?

**ALEX.** STOP.

(*pause*)

**WILL.** It's like—a blog. It's sort of a novel that I'm writing online.

**ALEX.** People read it?

**WILL.** Yeah.

**ALEX.** How many?

**WILL.** Quite a few. I don't know.

**ALEX.** What's it about?

(*no response*)

What's it about?

**WILL.** The Rapture.

(**ALEX** *stops writing, looks at* **WILL.** *Pause.*)

You actually know what that is?

(**LEROY** *enters. He glares at* **WILL** *and goes to his locker, taking out his vest.*)

**ALEX.** GO AWAY LEROY I'M DOING SOMETHING.

(**LEROY** *exits.*)

**WILL.** Do you want to be a composer?

(**ALEX** *considers for a second.*)

**ALEX.** Yeah. Kind of.

**WILL.** What instrument?

**ALEX.** It's not like that, it's like—performance art.

(*pause*)

You wouldn't understand.

**WILL.** No, but I'd like to.

**P.A. ANNOUNCMENT (PAULINE).** Will to register four, please. Will, register four.

**WILL.** Could you—could I hear some of it sometime? Do you have any recordings of your music, or—?

**ALEX.** People don't take me seriously. You wouldn't take me seriously.

**WILL.** I would. I take you seriously.

(**ALEX** *considers for a second, then takes out his iPod and some iPod speakers.*)

**ALEX.** Don't look at me.

**WILL.** Don't—?

**ALEX.** When I'm performing. Don't look at me.

**WILL.** Oh, you're going to—?

**ALEX.** My music isn't meant to be recorded.

**WILL.** You want to—here, right now?

**ALEX.** Yeah. Don't look at me.

**WILL.** Oh—uh, okay.

> (**WILL** *turns away from* **ALEX.** **ALEX** *searches around on his iPod for a second. He flips around in his notebook a bit, stopping at a page. He hits play on his iPod. A simple, electronic riff starts to play.*)

**ALEX.** I got this from a Casio keyboard made in 1989.

**WILL.** It's pretty.

**ALEX.** IT'S NOT SUPPOSED TO BE PRETTY.

**WILL.** Okay, I'm sorry. Sorry.

> (**ALEX** *takes a breath. After a moment,* **ALEX** *starts to read. It shouldn't be "singing" per se—but he obviously has very specific ideas on volume, tone, rhythm, etc that make the reading sound vaguely musical.*)

**ALEX.**

FEED YOUR USELESENESS

FEED YOUR USELESSNESS

CLOWN OF CLOWNS

NATION OF TEARS

I AM HUNGRY

I AM HUNGRY

CLOWN OF CLOWNS

NATION OF TEARS

I AM HUNGRY

I AM HUNGRY

(ants and bedbugs)

(ants and bedbugs)

BLOOD AND GUTS AND FLESH AND TRUTH

BLOOD AND GUTS AND FLESH AND LIES

CLOWN OF CLOWNS
NATION OF TEARS
(ants and bedbugs)
(ants and bedbugs)
I'M EATING TOO FAST
WE'RE EATING TOO FAST
WE'RE CHOKING
CHOKING
CHOKING
CHOKING
SWALLOW IT
CAPITALISM
END

*(The song ends abruptly,* **ALEX** *turns off the music right at the last lyric. Long pause.* **ALEX** *looks at* **WILL**.*)*

**ALEX.** You can look at me now.

*(***WILL*** looks at* **ALEX**, *not knowing what to say.)*

**ALEX.** It's deliberately ironic, it's a statement about consumerism, and—

*(pause)*

Fuck this, you don't get it. No one gets it.

**WILL.** No, it was… thank you. Thank you for doing that for me, that was—neat, it was—really interesting—

**ALEX.** Interesting? I'm gonna kill myself.

**P.A. ANNOUNCEMENT (PAULINE).** Will. Register four. Now.

*(***ALEX*** gets up.)*

**ALEX.** I'm going back to the floor now.

**WILL.** Wait—

*(***WILL*** blocks him from leaving.)*

**ALEX.** What are you doing? Stop.

**WILL.** Please, just—I just want to talk to you—

**ALEX.** Stop.

*(ALEX's breathing becomes quicker.)*

**WILL.** I just want to get to / know you—

**ALEX.** STOP. STOP.

**WILL.** I'm your father! / I just want to—

**ALEX.** STOP STOP STOP STOP

> *(ALEX, becoming more and more agitated, stands up, hyperventilating. He grabs his chest.)*

**WILL.** Okay, I'm sorry—what's the matter? Okay, just—calm down, you're okay—

> *(WILL wraps his arms around ALEX. PAULINE enters. She sees ALEX.)*

**PAULINE.** Fuck me. What did you say to him?

**WILL.** Nothing! I didn't say anything!

> *(PAULINE rushes to the phone, paging over the PA.)*

**PAULINE.** Leroy, breakroom now.

> *(ALEX gets worse and worse.)*

**WILL.** Alex, just take a breath. Take a breath, / you just need to breathe—

**PAULINE.** Leroy knows what to do, just get away from him.

**WILL.** Alex, it's alright. / Just calm down.

**PAULINE.** Goddammit, Will, I said leave him alone!

> *(LEROY enters. WILL still has ALEX in his arms, ALEX struggles a bit but WILL holds onto him.)*

**LEROY.** GET OFF HIM.

> *(WILL backs off of ALEX. ALEX slumps down to the floor, LEROY goes to him.)*

**LEROY.** Okay, buddy, you ready? Look right in my eyes.

> *(ALEX looks at him. They stare at one another silently for a very long time—finally, ALEX starts to shake a little less. Very slowly, his breathing starts to regulate. Finally, ALEX stops shaking and breathes normally, still looking straight at LEROY.)*

**ALEX.** Chagall?

**LEROY.** Nope. Kandinsky.

**ALEX.** It never works.

**LEROY.** One day.

*(Pause.* **LEROY** *helps him up.)*

**PAULINE.** Alex, take the rest of the day off, okay?

**LEROY.** *(to* **ALEX***)* You okay?

**ALEX.** Yeah.

**LEROY.** I'll drive you home—

**ALEX.** I have my bike. I'm fine.

**PAULINE.** You sure?

*(***ALEX** *gathers his things.)*

**ALEX.** Yeah.

*(pause)*

Sorry.

**PAULINE.** Nothing to be sorry for.

*(***ALEX** *exits, followed by* **LEROY***.)*

Fuck I hate it when he does that thing. He'll be fine. But if it happens again, don't fucking go near him, just get Leroy in here as fast as you can, okay?

**WILL.** Okay.

**PAULINE.** *(checking her clipboard)* Alright. Well, now we're sort of fucked, we only have two on front lines, and we've got that whole back-to-school display to—

*(***LEROY** *re-enters, going to* **WILL***.)*

**LEROY.** I told you to stay / away from him.

**WILL.** Leroy, honestly, / I didn't do anything, I didn't—

**PAULINE.** Leroy—

*(***LEROY** *gets in* **WILL***'s face, shoving him into the lockers.)*

**LEROY.** WHAT DID YOU SAY TO HIM?

*(***PAULINE** *rushes over to them, breaking them up.)*

**PAULINE.** OKAY OKAY OKAY ENOUGH.

(**LEROY** *moves away from* **WILL**. *Pause.*)

**PAULINE.** Both of you sit down. Now.

(**WILL** *and* **LEROY** *sit.* **PAULINE** *turns off the television and pulls out a conflict resolution form, begins to fill it out.*)

**PAULINE.** Fucking conflict resolution, I don't have time for fucking conflict resolution today.

**LEROY.** Do we have to do this, Pauline?

**PAULINE.** Fuck you, Leroy. Last year when that guy, what's his name, lazy eye, CARL—when Carl made Mandy cry and Mandy went to corporate and I had to do a FUCKING WEEKEND WORKSHOP, so yes, we have to do this. Alright. Let's just do this as fast as possible. Each of you, state your case or whatever. Leroy you go first.

**LEROY.** Sure.

**WILL.** I didn't do anything—

**PAULINE.** No interrupting. Leroy, go.

**WILL.** I really don't feel comfortable with—

**PAULINE.** FUCK YOU, WILL. Leroy, go. And try to phrase everything in terms of how you feel.

**LEROY.** I feel this is stupid.

**PAULINE.** I FEEL FUCK YOU LEROY.

**LEROY.** Pauline, do you know who this guy really is?

(*pause*)

**PAULINE.** What?

**LEROY.** He's from that crazy end-times church up outside of Couer d'Alene, in Rathdrum? The one from a few months ago, with the pastor who let that kid die out in the forest?

(*pause*)

**PAULINE.** (*to* **WILL**) You're in that church?

**WILL.** New Life Church doesn't even exist anymore, I was just a member of the congregation—

**LEROY.** You were like the second in command, you lived at the church–

**WILL.** No, see, this is something the papers all got wrong. I lived at the church because they paid me to be their bookkeeper and janitor. There were over ninety people in the congregation, I was just one of them.

*(pause)*

Pastor Rick is going to jail, and he has to live with the reality of what he did, and I—... I was questioned for months. I had nothing to do with Daniel Sharp's death.

*(Silence.* **PAULINE** *crumples up the conflict resolution form. She paces a bit.)*

**PAULINE.** Why the fuck am I always the last one to know what's happening in this store?

**LEROY.** Alex is his son. That he abandoned when Alex was a baby.

*(***PAULINE*** *drops her clipboard, exasperated. Silence. After a few moments,* **PAULINE** *collects herself.)*

**PAULINE.** Leroy, clock out and go home.

**LEROY.** Me?

**PAULINE.** LEROY.

*(***LEROY*** *angrily grabs his bag out of a locker and leaves the room.* **PAULINE** *stares at* **WILL.***)*

**WILL.** I didn't mean to cause trouble.

**PAULINE.** Be quiet.

*(pause)*

You know I can fire you.

**WILL.** I'm a good employee. I don't have a criminal record. You can't fire me because of a church I used to go to.

*(pause)*

**PAULINE.** I'm gonna say this once, and I hope you understand me.

*(pause)*

I took over this store four years ago.

**PAULINE.** *(cont.)* The first day I was here, four out of six cashiers called in sick, there were rats in the stock room, and a good quarter of all items on the floor were mis-stocked or mis-labeled. The manager before me, this little pip-squeak from Nampa, he saw there was mold problem in the air ducts so his solution was to puncture an air freshener and toss it inside. It was chaos, you understand? Corporate told me I was taking over as a temporary measure, to oversee the branch for six months before, they said, they would most likely close it completely. And what did I do? I cleaned it up. I stayed here during nights by myself restocking and organizing, cleaning the air ducts, firing and hiring and basically reshaping this entire store from the ground up. I took out ads in the paper announcing new management and grand-reopening sales. Six months later, our profits were up sixty-two percent, and they've been climbing ever since. I, Will, I brought order to chaos.

**WILL.** That's really—impressive.

**PAULINE.** Goddam right it's impressive. Damn near miraculous. And it happened because of me. Because I changed everything about this store, I changed the way this store feels, the way it thinks, the fucking ecosystem in this store. And I will not have you or anyone else disrupting the ecosystem I have painstakingly crafted.

*(pause)*

Listen, personally, I don't give a shit what you believe. But as far as the good people of Boise are concerned, you are a state-wide embarrassment. And if people were to find out that one of our cashiers is from this wacky little cult up north, they may think about buying their silk flowers somewhere else.

*(pause)*

When you're in this store, just—stay away from Alex, understand? And I don't want anyone else finding out about this church of yours. No customers, no co-workers, no one.

*(pause)*

You're on register four.

*(**WILL** gets up and starts to exit.)*

**PAULINE.** So you still believe in God?

*(Pause. **WILL** turns back to **PAULINE**.)*

**WILL.** Yes.

**PAULINE.** After all that?

**WILL.** Yes.

**PAULINE.** Why?

*(pause)*

**WILL.** You'll see.

*(**WILL** exits.)*

## Scene Seven.

*(Night.* **WILL**, *in the parking lot, as in scene one. Once again, the sounds of the freeway can be heard as well as the buzzing glow of neon signs and florescent lights overhead.)*

*(He stands with his eyes closed, listening to the noise.)*

**WILL.** Now.

...

...

...

Now.

*(silence, then becoming more aggressive)*

Now.

*(long pause, more aggressive)*

NOW.

*(pause, more aggressive still)*

NOW NOW NOW NOW NOW N—

**(WILL** *stops himself, opening his eyes. Pause.)*

*(The noise continues.)*

## Scene Eight.

*(That night. **WILL** sits in the breakroom, his computer hooked up to the internet jack on the wall. A video of a liposuction plays on the television.)*

*(**ANNA** enters, seeing **WILL**. She averts her eyes a bit, but doesn't leave. Long pause.)*

**WILL.** I can go.

**ANNA.** It's fine.

*(Short pause, then **ANNA** sits down at a table. She notices the TV.)*

**ANNA.** Oh my God. What is that?

**WILL.** Oh—I don't know, looks like—I don't even know.

**ANNA.** That's just disgusting.

**WILL.** You want me to turn it off?

**ANNA.** Yes. No. Yes. No, leave it on. Oh my God! Every time I come in here and it's playing these medical things—I just can't stop looking, you know? Oh my God that's disgusting.

*(Pause. **ANNA** smiles a bit at **WILL**, then opens her book.)*

**WILL.** Where were you hiding tonight?

**ANNA.** Textiles.

**WILL.** You were?

**ANNA.** Yes.

**WILL.** I was there, too.

**ANNA.** You were not!

**WILL.** I was, I was next to the back-to-school display, behind the school desk and the—

**ANNA.** Shut up.

**WILL.** What?

**ANNA.** Shut up!

**WILL.** I'm—what?

**ANNA.** I was right next to you!

**WILL.** You were?

**ANNA.** I was crouched behind the button kiosk! We were five feet away from each other!

**WILL.** Oh, wow.

**ANNA.** That's just creepy! Well that's just creepy. How did we not see each other?

**WILL.** I'm pretty quiet.

**ANNA.** So am I. Jesus, it's just so—!

**WILL.** Please don't—… Sorry.

**ANNA.** What?

**WILL.** It's just—I'm sorry, the swearing—it's…

**ANNA.** Oh. I'm so sorry.

**WILL.** It's fine—

**ANNA.** Sorry.

> (**ANNA** *almost goes back to reading, then:*)

> I just want to say I think it's really great that you're here to re-connect with a son, I think that's a great thing to do. I think that's very mature, and very sweet.

**WILL.** Thank you.

**ANNA.** I mean, uprooting yourself and moving here from— where are you from?

> (*pause*)

**WILL.** Up North.

**ANNA.** Up North, you move here from up north and you want to get to know your son, you want to re-unite? That's just great, it's really sweet.

**WILL.** Thank you.

> (*pause*)

**ANNA.** I'm sorry for swearing.

**WILL.** It's completely fine.

**ANNA.** It's such a bad habit. Working around Pauline, I think that's what does it. I start to sound like her.

**WILL.** You don't sound like her.

ANNA. I mean, I grew up Lutheran, my mother's very religious. And I go to church sometimes with her, I have respect for... You know, God, and everything. And like I said, I believe in Jesus.

(pause)

Do you go to a church here?

(pause)

WILL. I had a church up North, but I haven't really... I haven't found one here yet.

ANNA. Go to the Lutheran church!

WILL. Maybe.

ANNA. I don't mean to be forward, I'm sorry. Am I annoying you? You look like you want to get to work.

WILL. No, it's... I enjoy talking to you.

(ANNA blushes.)

ANNA. Oh, shut up, you shut up! You're cute.

WILL. And we both hid in textiles tonight, maybe we're kindred spirits.

ANNA. Oh, shut up!

(ANNA hits him with her book, maybe a little too hard.)

Oh my God, I'm sorry.

WILL. It's okay.

ANNA. And I just swore!

WILL. Yes, you did.

ANNA. I'm just sort of an idiot.

WILL. No, you're not.

ANNA. I really am, believe me. I think Pauline's ready to fire me.

WILL. Why?

ANNA. Oh, I just don't do anything right. I put the wrong barcode on an entire palette of doll heads the other day, do you believe that? I put the arm and leg barcode on every last one of them. Pauline says I cost the company over a hundred dollars.

**WILL.** You just made a mistake.

**ANNA.** Yeah, well, that's one thing I'm good at. I don't even want to tell you how many places I've been fired from in this city. Barnes & Noble, JCPenney, three McDonald's, two Wendy's, the Super Walmart and the regular Walmart—pretty soon I'm gonna run out. Have to go back to telemarketing, I really hate telemarketing.

**WILL.** Are you married?

*(pause)*

Sorry, what a dumb thing to just blurt out like that, I just—

**ANNA.** No, I'm not…I have a boyfriend. Well, sort of, we— you know, we date.

**WILL.** What does he do?

**ANNA.** He's a telemarketer.

*(quick pause)*

And you're a writer!

**WILL.** Not—really.

**ANNA.** Well, you write things and people read them, that makes you a writer, doesn't it? Like I said, it's probably better than this book here. I have to stick with it till it's done, but it's just so awful. It's called "Falling From Grace." You ever read it?

**WILL.** No.

**ANNA.** The main character's called "Grace," get it?

**WILL.** Oh, sure.

**ANNA.** She lives on this big estate in California, and she has this really rich husband, but all of a sudden he dies in this big car wreck, and turns out that— I'm sorry, what am I doing?

**WILL.** No, no—keep going.

**ANNA.** Well, she has to figure out how to live now that she doesn't have this rich husband, and turns out he had all this debt, so she didn't get any money, and then she has to move into this studio apartment and it's hard and blah blah blah. Anyhoo! She's working as a check-out girl, and she falls in love with a customer, and they end up together, and she's happy. And now I'm fifteen pages from the end, so I'm hoping she dies.

*(pause)*

**WILL.** Wait, I'm sorry, you hope she—?

**ANNA.** Well c'mon! Why the heck have I read a hundred and eighty pages? To hear about this woman getting married and being happy? This is what I'm reading?! I heard once about that book called Anna—something. Anna Karenia? Is that it? Anyway it's this old Russian novel, someone told me she kills herself at the end and that sounded good but it just looked so long.

*(pause)*

Does anyone die in your book?

**WILL.** Well, it's—about the end of the world, actually.

**ANNA.** Oh my gosh, a lot of people die then!

**WILL.** Yeah, quite a few.

**ANNA.** That sounds so good!

**WILL.** Thank you.

**ANNA.** Read some to me! Is that okay that I said that? I'm sorry.

**WILL.** Oh, well—it's online, you can just—

**ANNA.** Oh, we don't have a computer at the house. Well, we do, but my dad is the only one who uses it, he doesn't…

*(pause)*

If you don't wanna read it to me, that's fine. I'm being annoying.

**WILL.** No, you're not, it's me—I just sort of feel like I've lost faith in what I'm writing.

**ANNA.** Oh, well, all writers hate their own writing, isn't that a thing?

**WILL.** Yeah, well. Okay, I can…

*(scrolling on the computer screen)*

This is funny, I'm a little nervous.

**ANNA.** You're nervous because of me?

**WILL.** A little.

**ANNA.** Oh shut up. That's so cute! I'm sorry, that's just so cute, shut up.

*(pause)*

**WILL.** Okay.

*(reading)*

"When Andy woke up that morning to his screeching alarm clock, he knew that something was different. The bedroom in his small apartment was windowless but the darkness he woke up to that morning felt more profound, more deliberate. And as he stumbled his way to the light-switch, his forehead sweating, somehow he knew something greater was happening. The light switch didn't work. He opened his bedroom door and squinted his eyes, expecting to greeted by the same blast of sunshine that hit his face every morning, but felt nothing, and saw nothing."

*(stops)*

Wow this is just terrible, isn't it? It sounds terrible when I read it out loud.

**ANNA.** No, it's not at all!  Keep going!

**WILL.** *(reading)* "His living room was pitch black as well. He fumbled through the darkness, barely able to make out the shape of the front door. 'It must still be night,' he thought to himself. 'Something must be wrong with my clock.' He managed to open the front door, and looking outside he saw—nothing. No sun, no moon, no stars. A blackness had overtaken everything. On a usual morning Andy would open his door to the street and the McDonald's and the Home Depot he lived next to. But today, there was no traffic. There were no billboards and neon signs.

**WILL.** *(cont.)* The whole buzz to the world had been taken away, apart from the faint sound of thousands upon thousands of people wandering the streets of the entire suburb, begging for light, cursing heaven, chewing their tongues, and at that moment Andy lifted his eyes to God and whispered an unconscious prayer of confusion, relief, and optimism."

*(long pause)*

**ANNA.** Holy crap. You really wrote that?

**WILL.** Yeah.

**ANNA.** That was so good!

**WILL.** It sounds so terrible to read it out loud—

**ANNA.** That sounds like a real book! Will, that totally sounds like a real book! That is a real book!

**WILL.** Thank you.

**ANNA.** I just… WOW!

*(staring at **WILL**)*

What are you doing working at a place like this? Why don't you get it published, make some money?

**WILL.** Oh, it's—sort of complicated—

**ANNA.** Do you need an agent for that kind of thing? I guess I don't know how all of this works. But you could get an agent, it's so good.

**WILL.** I never really did this for money, it wasn't about that.

**ANNA.** Oh, sure. You just love writing, / you're an artist.

**WILL.** I did it because I thought I was spreading God's word.

*(pause)*

**ANNA.** Huh?

**WILL.** Nothing, nevermind.

*(Pause. **ANNA** tenses up.)*

**ANNA.** So what kind of church did you go to?

*(pause)*

**WILL.** I'd actually rather not talk about it—

**ANNA.** Yeah but what kind of church was it?

**WILL.** It was a non-denominational—

**ANNA.** No, I mean like Methodist, Lutheran, whatever—

**WILL** That's what I'm saying, it was non-denominational. Nevermind, it doesn't—

**ANNA.** I don't know what that means.

**WILL.** It means that we weren't part of any huge network or organization, we started just because we wanted to. Because we didn't want a church dedicated to any organization, we just wanted a church dedicated to Christ.

*(pause)*

**ANNA.** I'm Lutheran.

**WILL.** Oh.

**ANNA.** Yeah. I only go sometimes. *(pause)* You don't know me.

*(pause)*

**WILL.** What?

**ANNA.** I said you don't know me.

**WILL.** I didn't say that I—

**ANNA.** You know I've had a lot of co-workers like you, super religious guys who try to get me to go to church with them, these little whattayoucallthem, evangelical churches? I even went a couple times. They'd see me sitting and reading my books or whatever, and they'd think, now there's someone who needs help. But let me tell you, I don't need any help, and these churches? No different from a fucking Hobby Lobby, I'll tell you that much. Everyone wants something. So don't think that you know me.

**WILL.** I'm really not—I'm sorry. I'm not trying to convert you, believe me.

**ANNA.** You're not?

**WILL.** No. Really. I'd rather just—not talk about it.

*(pause)*

**ANNA.** Well what the hell? I'm not good enough for your church or something?

**WILL.** No, it's... I'm just gonna take off, I think.

*(**WILL** closes his computer, putting it into the case. He stands and is about to exit when:)*

**ANNA.** Sorry. It's not you. I know I can turn on a dime like that, I'm sorry. I live with my dad, and all my brothers, they make fun of me, especially when I read so... Anyway, I'm not good with people.

*(**WILL** goes back and sits next to **ANNA.**)*

Just do me a favor, okay? If you see God coming again, if you see him coming in his cloud or whatever and he's about to kill us unbelievers, you let me know, cause I'll be down on my hands and knees praying for forgiveness then, okay?

*(The television goes to static for a split second and then starts playing Hobby Lobby TV. They both look at it.)*

**WILL.** I thought someone had to jiggle the satellite dish.

**ANNA.** Sometimes it just flips back on. Thing has a mind of its own.

*(pause)*

I think I'm gonna go. It's nothing you said, just... Do you want to leave together? I'm not saying—Oh, gosh, I didn't mean—

**WILL.** No, it's fine, I—think I'll just stick around for a while longer.

**ANNA.** How much sleep do you get?

**WILL.** Lately, not much.

*(**WILL** goes back to his computer, opening it up. **ANNA** starts to exit.)*

**ANNA.** Maybe one of these nights I could try and read your book. Sometimes I can use the computer after my dad falls asleep.

*(They smile at one another.* **ANNA** *exits.* **WILL** *looks at his computer for a few moments, then closes it.)*

*(He turns on the television, Hobby Lobby TV is on. He puts a chair in front of the television and watches it silently.)*

## Scene Nine.

*(Hours later, the middle of the night, in the parking lot. The noise of the interstate is heard. ALEX is waiting in the shadows. WILL enters.)*

**ALEX.** Hi.

**WILL.** *(startled)* OH. My— Hi.

**ALEX.** Hi.

**WILL.** What are you—?

**ALEX.** I've been sitting out here for a while. I heard Villa-Lobos, were you playing Villa-Lobos in the breakroom?

**WILL.** Yeah.

**ALEX.** You know I don't even really like Villa-Lobos all that much.

**WILL.** You don't?

**ALEX.** Not really. I think it's sort of trite.

**WILL.** Oh. I... I really like it.

*(pause)*

How did you know I was—?

**ALEX.** Anna told me you've been spending your nights here.

*(pause)*

**WILL.** I'm sorry if I did something wrong earlier today, I didn't mean for you to get upset—

**ALEX.** Leroy told me about that church you used to go to. He said you guys called yourselves "evangelical", but he said that's just a code word for a cult.

**WILL.** It wasn't a cult.

**ALEX.** So what was it?

*(no reply)*

My best friend and I used to write music together, all the time. But then he started going to one of those evangelical churches. He said he didn't need music anymore, he said he was happier than music could ever make him. And I'd ask him to tell me about his church, but he said he couldn't talk to me anymore because I was ruining his relationship with God. He doesn't even look at me now. We're in English together, first period, and every fucking morning he looks so happy.

*(pause)*

Tell me what your church was like. Go.

**WILL.** That church doesn't exist anymore. We don't need to talk about it.

**ALEX.** Tell me or I'm going home. *(pause)* Go.

*(pause)*

**WILL.** In the beginning, it was—amazing. We were all young and ambitious, we would sit around with one another for hours, studying the Bible and talking about our lives—we started a church from the ground up. We weren't interested in emulating any other church, we wanted to create something that was—brand new. And we did. It was—

**ALEX.** STOP. *(pause)* If your church was so amazing, why did that kid die?

**WILL.** We don't need to talk about / that—

**ALEX.** Leroy told me the story, but I want to hear it from you.

**WILL.** Why?

**ALEX.** Because if you do, I'll tell you some things about me. *(pause)* Go.

*(pause)*

**WILL.** Danny was—…He had just graduated from high school. His parents wanted him to go to school and become a pharmacist, he didn't want to leave the congregation. They basically disowned him. I lived at the church, and since we both worked at the same Albertson's, it just made sense for him to live there too.

**ALEX.** You lived together?

**WILL.** Yes. He was looking for spiritual guidance, and in a way, so was I. He didn't want to be a pharmacist, I didn't want to work at Albertson's. We helped one another.

*(pause)*

One night, after work, Danny and I were in the Albertson's parking lot, and he told me that he—was questioning his faith, that he didn't believe in God. I didn't know what to do, I was in over my head. So I went to our pastor, and—I told him what Danny had said to me.

**ALEX.** You told on him. *(pause)* Then what happened?

**WILL.** You already know the rest of the story—

**ALEX.** Tell me what happened next. Go.

*(pause)*

**WILL.** Rick took him into the wilderness. He thought he could help Danny gain an understanding of his place in God's universe if he—brought him to a point of physical exhaustion. He felt that God was telling him to do it.

*(pause)*

**ALEX.** Keep going.

**WILL.** About a week later, Pastor Rick comes back to the church, and he comes to me and says—he says he has Danny in the trunk of his car, and he doesn't know what to do. He says that a day earlier he woke up and Danny was stiff. And blue. And he tried to perform CPR, but it didn't work. And he started to cry, and I called the police.

*(pause)*

Yes, I told on Danny. I told on him and if I would have known that Rick was capable of…I pray for forgiveness every night, every night I—

**ALEX.** I was molested by my sixth grade teacher.

*(pause)*

Also, I was raped by my fourth grade teacher.

**WILL.** You were–?

**ALEX.** And my fifth and third and second grade teachers.

**WILL.** What are you doing?

**ALEX.** When I was thirteen I was kidnapped for over a week. I was blindfolded in the trunk of a car, every eight hours they would open it up and feed me and give me water without taking the blindfold off.

**WILL.** Wait——

**ALEX.** When I was eight, I was camping with my parents and wandered off, and they found me over a month later, and they still don't know how I survived, and I don't remember any of it.

When I was fifteen, I watched my best friend commit suicide with his dad's old army pistol. All my life, my parents have told me that I'm not important because I'm not their real kid.

*(pause)*

**WILL.** I don't underst——

**ALEX.** The thing about being raped in the fourth grade I told Pauline when she first hired me. The thing about my friend committing suicide is something I told Anna. The thing about being kidnapped, I told that to my biology teacher. I got an A this semester.

**WILL.** So none of / that is——

**ALEX.** The last one about my parents, I told to Leroy. He's confronted my parents about it before, they always deny it. But he believes me.

*(silence)*

**WILL.** Why did you tell me all that?

**ALEX.** Because you told me about Daniel Sharp.

*(pause)*

**WILL.** The story about your friend, the friend who joined a church and stopped talking to you—that one's true?

**ALEX.** That one's true. I haven't told anyone that. Not even Leroy.

**WILL.** Was he a good friend?

**ALEX.** He was my only friend.

(*pause*)

**WILL.** You don't have any songs you wrote by yourself?

**ALEX.** I wrote all my songs with him.                        '

**WILL.** You don't have any songs you wrote by yourself?

**ALEX.** I don't know. I guess. (*pause*) They're dumb.

**WILL.** I'd really love to hear one. If you—if that's alright.

**ALEX.** What, right here?

(**ALEX** *considers for a minute, then starts flipping through his notebook. He lands on a page, looks at it for a second.*)

**ALEX.** I've—…I've got one, but I've barely even looked at it. No one's heard it.

**WILL.** That's great.

**ALEX.** I haven't even set it to music yet.

**WILL.** That's fine, just—read it to me. You don't need music.

**ALEX.** It's stupid. It's not like, my real art, it's just something stupid I wrote.

**WILL.** I don't care. I'd just love to hear you read it.

(**ALEX** *hesitates for a second, then reads.*)

**ALEX.** (*reading, meek and self-conscious*)
"My mind folds into itself
when you pass me
like I'm a dead man pretending to be asleep
like I'm a weed growing into itself
and you pass by me
you're passing by me
just now—
Ah, we once found ourselves
spread out onto the wet grass
in the night."

*(long pause)*

**ALEX.** *(cont.)* It's stupid, I don't know why I read this to you. It's not like my other stuff, it's trite and sentimental and stupid and—

**WILL.** That was overwhelming.

*(WILL smiles at ALEX, near tears. Pause.)*

**ALEX.** You still believe in God?

*(Pause. WILL looks away.)*

**WILL.** Yes.

**ALEX.** A God that let Daniel Sharp die in the forest?

**WILL.** Yes.

**ALEX.** Why?

*(pause)*

**WILL.** Because without God, then all I am is a terrible father who works in a Hobby Lobby and lives in his car. There are—greater things in life. There have to be.

*(Pause. ALEX shuts his notebook, putting it back in his backpack.)*

**ALEX.** Keep going.

### Scene Ten.

*(The next day.* **LEROY** *sits in the breakroom reading a book, wearing a T-shirt that reads "YOU WILL EAT YOUR CHILDREN." * **ALEX** *enters, not looking at* **LEROY**.*)*

**LEROY.** Hey.

**ALEX.** Hi.

*(***ALEX** *puts his things in a locker, is about to head out.)*

**LEROY.** Why didn't you want a ride this morning?

**ALEX.** You didn't get my text?

**LEROY.** No, I got it. But why didn't you need a ride?

**ALEX.** Felt like riding my bike. Is that a new shirt?

**LEROY.** Made it a few weeks ago. You like it? I can make you one.

**ALEX.** It's sort of overdone. The font is too aggressive.

**LEROY.** Wow. Okay then.

**ALEX.** I'm just being honest. You want me to lie? Fine. Leroy, it's amazing, you're fucking Picasso.

*(***ALEX** *is about to head out to the floor.)*

**LEROY.** Hold up a sec.

**ALEX.** I'm gonna be late clocking in.

**LEROY.** Two minutes.

*(***ALEX** *sighs, comes back in.)*

Mom called me. She said you snuck out last night. I covered, I told her you came over to my apartment.

**ALEX.** I don't care what your mom thinks.

**LEROY.** So what'd you do? Get drunk with friends?

**ALEX.** What friends?

**LEROY.** Is it a girl?

**ALEX.** Leroy, cut it out.

**LEROY.** Were you with this guy? Your dad, whatever? Please tell me you weren't with that guy. *(no response)* Jesus, Alex.

**ALEX.** It's not a big deal. We just talked.

**LEROY.** About what?

**ALEX.** I asked him about the church he was in and stuff.

**LEROY.** What did he say?

**ALEX.** I don't know. I have to clock in.

**LEROY.** Seriously, what did he say? Did he tell you about how the earth is six-thousand years old, or that dinosaurs co-existed with man, or—

**ALEX.** You know, that kid up in Rathdrum—it wasn't really his fault.

*(pause)*

**LEROY.** Okay—yeah, I know it wasn't his fault, I didn't... *(pause)* Alex—you know this guy is nuts, right?

**ALEX.** Would you stop it? You have no idea what this is like for me, okay?

**LEROY.** Oh great, are we doing the poor orphan routine now?

*(pause)*

**ALEX.** Maybe he has some interesting things to say, did you ever think about that? No, because you're always right, and people who believe different things than you are just stupid, right? Maybe I like hearing about that stuff. Maybe I'm interested, how about that?

*(**ANNA** enters. She starts to put her things into a locker.)*

**ALEX.** Hi, Anna.

**ANNA.** Morning. Watch out for Pauline, she just chewed me out for coming in four minutes late.

**LEROY.** *(to **ALEX**)* So what are you saying? You're gonna like—get baptized, or something?

**ALEX.** I DIDN'T SAY THAT, I JUST SAID—you know, forget it. Anna, I like that shirt.

**ANNA.** Oh, thanks!

**LEROY.** No, seriously. You want to be a Christian, is that it?

**ALEX.** I don't know! Why can't I just talk to him about it?!

**LEROY.** Because he's a fucking psycho! And he might be dangerous!

**ALEX.** Anna, do you think Will is dangerous?

**ANNA.** Dangerous? Why would he be dangerous?

(**WILL** *enters.*)

**LEROY.** *(to* **WILL***)* What did you do with him last night?

**ALEX.** Leroy—

**WILL.** I—we didn't do anything—

**LEROY.** I want you to keep away from him, you understand me?

**WILL.** He came to me, I didn't—

**ALEX.** Leroy, back off!

**LEROY.** WHY ARE YOU DEFENDING HIM? AM I THE ONLY SANE PERSON LEFT IN THIS STORE? You know what, fuck this, I'm taking care of all right now.

(**LEROY** *goes to the phone and dials a few numbers, putting himself over the P.A.*)

**LEROY.** *(into the PA system)* Attention Hobby Lobby employees / and guests.

**ALEX.** Leroy, stop!

**LEROY.** *(staring straight at* **WILL***)* This is just a friendly announcement to let you know that one of our new employees, Will Cronin, was directly involved with the scandal with the cult up north that killed a kid out in the forest. He's an unapologetic religious fanatic, and he believes that soon—

(**PAULINE** *enters furiously.*)

—Jesus will come again and kill everyone who doesn't share his fucked up beliefs and—

(**PAULINE** *heads straight for the phone, hanging it up with her finger. She stares at* **LEROY***.*)

Fuck this. Alex, come on.

(**ALEX** *doesn't move.*)

**LEROY.** ALEX C'MON.

(*Again,* **ALEX** *doesn't move.* **PAULINE** *whips out a keychain, and in one swift motion, locks the door.*)

**LEROY.** Pauline.

(**PAULINE,** *desperately containing her rage, paces over to the lockers.* **LEROY** *tries the door, it doesn't open.*)

**LEROY.** Pauline, unlock the / fucking door—

**PAULINE.** SHUT UP SHUT UP SHUT UP. No one's leaving. No one's quitting, just shut up. I just need to—FUCK. I need to think. I just need to think for a minute. Everyone sit down.

(*no one moves*)

EVERYONE SIT DOWN NOW.

(*Everyone sits.*)

(*nearly frantic*) Is it too much to ask that we have a normal fucking workday around here?! Here's a news flash for all of you. What people believe doesn't fucking matter. What matters are real things. Real things like money, the economy, and a country so beautiful that it can support a chain of big box retail stores that makes all its money off of selling people quilting supplies and construction paper. That is what matters.

(*pause, thinking*)

Alright, there's only one way to deal with this. Will, I'm sorry—you can finish out the rest of your day, but after that you're gonna have to find work somewhere else.

**WILL.** What exactly am I being / fired for?

**PAULINE.** Look around! One week ago, this store was doing just fine, and now it's fucking chaos! Alex is my most accurate cashier, Leroy knows more about art supplies than anyone in this entire company. It's either them or you. It's my fault, I should have called your references, that's for damn sure.

(*pause*)

Alright, here's what were gonna do. Anna, go out to the floor. Tell any customer you see that a teenager got on the PA or something.

(**PAULINE** *unlocks the door.*)

**ANNA.** Oh—uh, I don't—

**PAULINE.** ANNA GO NOW.

(**ANNA** *exits.*)

Will, register three. (*pause*) Please.

(*Pause.* **WILL** *considers, then finally makes his way back to the floor.*)

Alright, I need both of you back out on the floor. There's four palettes out there that need to be stocked—

**LEROY.** We need a minute. Please, just a minute.

(**PAULINE** *relents and exits.* **LEROY** *nods.* **PAULINE** *exits. Silence.*)

**ALEX.** You think I'm stupid.

**LEROY.** No—

**ALEX.** You think I'm a child.

**LEROY.** ALEX. (*pause*) Look, I just—… If you wanna be a—Christian, or whatever—

**ALEX.** Would you stop? It's not about that, it's… (*pause*) Leroy, what the fuck does the rest of my life look like?

**LEROY.** What? Where is this coming from?

**ALEX.** Last night he told me that life was meaningless. That the reason that he believed in God was that everything on earth was meaningless.

**LEROY.** And you believe that?

**ALEX.** Maybe. (*pause*) In less than a year, I'm gonna graduate. What the hell am I gonna do then?

**LEROY.** You have a plan. You'll go to BSU, if the financial aid doesn't come through—

**ALEX.** That's your plan, not mine. And even if I do that, go to school and major in music, then what? You think I'm gonna like, be the next fucking big thing?

**LEROY.** Why not?

**ALEX.** Okay, so I make a few albums, do some performances, probably wind up teaching or something, and
that's like, the best case scenario.

*(getting upset)*

What's most likely going to happen is that I'm going
to be mediocre or fail completely at it, come back
to Boise, and end up working at this fucking Hobby
Lobby—

**LEROY.** Okay, calm down.

**ALEX.** —working at this fucking store, for the rest of my life,
and that sounds pretty meaningless to me. And what's
the alternative? Believing in what my dad believes in,
believing in some magical guy up in the clouds who
created us for fun I guess, a guy who is going to come
pretty soon to kill us all. And that's just as meaningless.
These are my two options in life, and they are fucking
meaningless.

**LEROY.** *(cold)* OKAY ALEX.

*(**ALEX** stops. Silence.)*

Look, just—… Buddy, I wish I could give you some big
answer, but the truth is we all just do the best we can.

*(pause)*

**ALEX.** Think of one.

*(pause)*

**LEROY.** Right now?

**ALEX.** Yeah.

**LEROY.** No, Alex, c'mon.

**ALEX.** I just feel like it, let's just try. C'mon.

*(pause)*

**LEROY.** Uh. Okay, I got one.

*(**LEROY** looks into **ALEX**'s eyes. Silence. **ALEX** stares into
his eyes for a long moment.)*

**ALEX.** Frida Kahlo.

*(pause)*

**LEROY.** Nope. It's—

**ALEX.** DON'T TELL ME. *(pause)* Pollack.

*(**LEROY** shakes his head.)*

**ALEX.** Rauschenberg.

**LEROY.** No—

**ALEX.** Edward Hopper. Georgia O'Keefe.

**LEROY.** Alex, enough. You're not gonna get it. *(pause)* You wanna keep working, or you wanna go home?

*(silence)*

**ALEX.** I wanna go home.

**LEROY.** Okay. Just give me a minute, I'll go talk to Pauline and then I'll take you home, alright?

*(**LEROY** exits. **ALEX** sits motionless for a second, then looks at Hobby Lobby TV. He sits for a long moment listening to the television, before standing up and turning up the volume. For the first time the voices are discernible. The two men speak very slowly, nearly in a monotone.)*

**HOBBY LOBBY TV (MALE 1).** —and so it's, uh. Yeah, it's I think—what's the retail on this?

**HOBBY LOBBY TV (MALE 2).** It's, uh—

**HOBBY LOBBY TV (MALE 1).** It's really a great / product, you know—

**HOBBY LOBBY TV (MALE 2).** It's ninety-seven.

**HOBBY LOBBY TV (MALE 1).** What's that?

**HOBBY LOBBY TV (MALE 2).** Ninety-seven cents. The unit, it's uh. Ninety-seven.

**HOBBY LOBBY TV (MALE 1).** Oh, see and that's—that's down from last year. That same unit, uhhh… That was, I wanna say a dollar ten last year. But we, you know. We talked with our distributor, and he—

*(Slowly, **ALEX** sits down, keeping his eyes on the television.)*

**HOBBY LOBBY TV (MALE 2).** It's always nice when we can offer these savings.

**HOBBY LOBBY TV (MALE 1).** Yeah, it's. It's good to, you know, point the customers toward savings like these. It's a good thing for our employees to keep in mind. I'll tell you, you know, it's also. It's a good product. It's really—you can really do a lot with something like this. Kids love it, and it's good for kids—they can be so creative with things like this—

**HOBBY LOBBY TV (MALE 2).** Durable, too.

**HOBBY LOBBY TV (MALE 1).** Oh, yeah. You know, it's popular during back to school, it's. Teachers, you know, art teachers, they pick these up—school districts, they love these, and it's great / when we—

**HOBBY LOBBY TV (MALE 2).** This year, for the first time, we've been sending fliers out to individual school districts, and we've been getting a great response. The teachers uh, appreciate it.

(**ALEX** *continues to watch, becoming more and more upset. His breathing becomes quicker.*)

**HOBBY LOBBY TV (MALE 2).** This is, uh. Store number 1478 in Cedar Rapids, they sent out some fliers to the local school board, and they said they've seen an increase in sales, uh, a four percent increase. For the Fall quarter, four percent. Really good stuff.

**HOBBY LOBBY TV (MALE 1).** Well, and you know, when you offer quality products like this, uh. You can—feel proud that we can serve our own community by giving them products like these at such low prices.

**HOBBY LOBBY TV (MALE 2).** And that we're helping these kids in their education—art is so important for these kids to learn at an early age, that's really what. It's something this company, it's founded on that.

(*For a moment, it looks like* **ALEX** *is having another panic attack—but this changes into a quieter, deeper grief.*)

**HOBBY LOBBY (MALE 1).** And you wanna give kids the best art supplies without going bankrupt.

**HOBBY LOBBY TV (MALE 2).** Yeah, exactly. / So this is—

**HOBBY LOBBY TV (MALE 1).** This is—yep, this is really just a solid product, great for art classes.

*(pause)*

Another great product here—you see this?

**HOBBY TV (MALE 2).** Oh yeah.

**HOBBY LOBBY TV (MALE 1).** We had this on the shelves down in store 1089 in Tallahassee—

*(LEROY enters.)*

**HOBBY LOBBY TV (MALE 1).** / —and it was off the shelves almost immediately, so we started introducing it nation wide starting last year.

**LEROY.** She says she'll want you to make up the hours this weekend. Mandy's off. *(pause)* You ready?

**HOBBY LOBBY TV (MALE 2).** We've been getting, uh. A really—a good response to the item, especially in our southeastern division, midwest division—

*(ALEX gets up, turning the volume back to its original level. ALEX looks at LEROY for a moment, then exits. LEROY follows him.)*

### Scene Eleven.

(*Much later that night.* **WILL,** *looking tired and worn out, stares at the television which plays an extreme close-up of eye surgery.*)

(**ANNA** *enters with a book. She sees* **WILL** *immediately.* **WILL** *continues to stare at the television. Not knowing exactly what to do,* **ANNA** *sits down at a table at the other side of the room and starts to read.*)

**WILL.** Why are you here so late?

**ANNA.** Couldn't sleep. I don't live far. Just thought I'd— finish up my book.

**WILL.** How'd you get in?

**ANNA.** I stole Pauline's spare key ring this afternoon. Got tired of hiding. I figure if she finds out, who cares, I'll go work somewhere else. This place is kinda boring anyway. (*looking at the TV*) Oh, gosh, that's an eye, isn't it?

**WILL.** Yeah. I think so.

(**ANNA** *moves over to him and sits with him.* **WILL** *finally looks at* **ANNA.**)

**ANNA.** I read that book of yours. Story, whatever it is.

(*pause*)

**WILL.** All of it?

**ANNA.** Not all of it. It's long, I didn't have time to read all of it. I had to sneak into my dad's room to use the computer, he was asleep in front of the TV. I didn't have a lot of time. It's really good.

(*pause*)

Listen, I know what getting fired feels like. I know. But there are plenty of other places in town you can get a job. My friend Ally, she just got a job at the Costco in Eagle, I could call her and—

**WILL.** I don't care about getting fired.

*(pause)*

**ANNA.** Oh. *(pause)* Then what's / the—

**WILL.** Alex came here last night, to see me. And he asked me about God, and the church, and I thought, this is—so amazing, God is giving me the opportunity to have a relationship with my son through him. We talked for hours out on the loading dock, and then we watched the sun come up over the highway. He promised me that he would meet me here again tonight. He called me toward the end of my shift, he told me he never wanted to see me again, and he hung up.

*(pause)*

I think I might be a bad person.

*(Pause. Slowly, **ANNA** goes to **WILL**, wrapping her arms around him in a hug. It's awkward at first, but eventually they settle into it.)*

**ANNA.** You know what part of your book I liked best? I mean, I haven't read the whole thing yet, but you know what part I really liked?

*(pause)*

**WILL.** What's that?

*(**ANNA** breaks the hug, but they remain close.)*

**ANNA.** There was that part with the pilot—what's his name?

**WILL.** Mark.

**ANNA.** Yeah! Mark. And Mark was flying over Israel and suddenly he looks out the window and he sees the, uh—the / four—

**WILL.** Four horsemen of the apocalypse.

**ANNA.** Yeah, and he knows that the world is gonna end, like, soon. And he thinks back on his life, and he realizes all of the bad things he's done, all of the sex and drugs and lies and whatever, and he all he wishes is that he could have repented everything in time. But it was too late. And then he dies. And no one can help him. *(pause)* Anyway, that was my favorite part.

*(pause)*

**WILL.** Danny and I worked at the same Albertson's, we'd try to get the same shifts so we could drive to work together. Some nights, we would both have closing shifts, be there until after midnight. And we'd hide in the store until everyone had left, and then in the middle of the night we'd would go out into the parking lot, right near I-90 where it's nothing but stores and parking lots and stuff. The last time I saw him we were standing in the parking lot praying for Christ to come again. We prayed for all of it to go away, we prayed for all of it to be swallowed up in divine fire, every disgusting house and parking lot and interstate and car and person on fire turning into ash and reforming as a city of pure light that was brilliant and eternal and unchanging and we prayed dear Jesus now.

...

...

...

Now.

...

...

...

Now.

...

...

...

Now.

...

...

...

And then nothing happened.

*(long silence)*

**ANNA.** Would you like to go to church with me on Sunday?

*(Pause.* **WILL** *looks at her.)*

**ANNA.** Look, I don't meet a lot of guys, and the ones I do meet are pretty much terrible. But you come in here at night just like I do, and you're such a talented writer, and I... And listen, you're not the only one with a checkered past, okay? When I dropped out of high school, I—... Anyway, I don't even need to tell you, let's just say that my father, he has good reason to be the overbearing asshole that he is. But I just think if you could come to church with me, if we could go together... The pastor, his name is Edward, but everyone calls him Pastor Eddie, it's really nice. And it's not all about hell and sin and whatever, it's just a nice community organization. They're very open-minded, we even have a gay couple that comes to our church, and no one even thinks twice about it. We have a food bank, and a youth group, and—...

*(pause)*

Will, you can just believe in something else!

**WILL.** Believe in what? Believe in the Lutheran Church, some branch of some branch of some branch of Christianity, some organization that's going to legislate my belief system instead of looking to God's word for it? You work at a Hobby Lobby, Anna. Before that you worked at Walmart, JC Penney, McDonald's, Barnes & Noble, and now we both work here. Your life is meaningless, my life is meaningless, and the only thing that gives any meaning, that brings any hope to this life is my unshakeable belief that God will come again in glory to replace this disgusting life with something new, and pure, and meaningful—

**ANNA.** Okay, Will.

**WILL.** *(rising)* And you could take the easy route, you could go to a liberal church, and believe in nothing, believe that God is unknowable and we'll never know the meaning of life, you'll go to college and get a degree in English or Philosophy or Art or Economics and you'll spend your life searching in the dark, trying to find meaning in meaninglessness—become one of those people who sit around in their fashionable clothes with their fashionable friends and call us bigots, and fanatics, and hicks, calling us idiots for actually believing in something, for standing for truth—

**ANNA.** Will, stop!

**WILL.** *(losing himself)* AND THESE PEOPLE WILL BURN IN HELL, YOU WILL BURN IN HELL BECAUSE INSTEAD OF SEEKING TRUTH YOU MOCK IT, YOU INSULT IT, YOU SPIT IN THE FACE OF GOD AND HE WILL—

*(With a quick burst of static, the television flips back to Hobby Lobby TV.* **WILL** *stops, looking at television. Pause.)*

*(***ANNA*** takes her book and exits.)*

*(***WILL*** watches the television for a moment, then slowly opens his laptop. He sits down, looks at the screen, and for the first time, begins to type.)*

## Scene Twelve.

*(Later that same night, in the parking lot. **WILL** stands, bathed in florescent light, listening to the interstate. **LEROY** enters behind him.)*

**LEROY.** Hey.

*(**WILL** turns around. Pause.)*

You know, last year I found Alex alone in his room reading a Bible. And I was actually angry. I was surprised, I didn't know I felt that strongly. I mean, I always knew that religion was bullshit, I just didn't...

*(pause)*

When he was little, I used to show him art films. Take him to galleries. I gave him the collected Ginsberg on his thirteenth birthday. And then seeing him sitting there reading that thing—it was like someone had invaded my turf.

**WILL.** You won't believe me when I say this, but I never intended on talking to him about what I believe, or my church, or... I just wanted to be his dad, I just—

**LEROY.** This afternoon he swallowed an entire bottle of my mom's sleeping pills. He's okay, they pumped his stomach. Doctors said he should be sent to some kind of juvenile mental health facility, something like that. Where he won't be a danger to himself. He won't talk to mom or dad. When I asked him why he did it, he said, "Hell is all around us."

*(pause)*

Get in my truck.

*(pause)*

**WILL.** What?

**LEROY.** You wanna be his dad? Now's your chance. We're going to the hospital, and you're going to talk to him. You're going to tell him that there's no heaven, no hell, no apocalypse. No God.

*(pause)*

WILL. I'm—I'm sorry—

LEROY. You have a choice right now, do you understand? You can go on believing in this bullshit, or you can give it up right now, and maybe—someday—have a normal relationship with your son. *(pause)* Well?

*(WILL, holding back tears, looks away from LEROY. He closes his eyes.)*

WILL. Now.

LEROY. What are you doing?

*(long silence)*

WILL. Now.

*(WILL doesn't move. Finally, LEROY exits. WILL looks back to the interstate, standing in the light in the same way he did at the beginning of the play. Long pause as he listens. He closes his eyes.)*

WILL. Now.

...

...

...

Now.

*(The sounds of the interstate start to grow in volume.)*

WILL. Now.

*(The florescent lights become brighter.)*

WILL. Now.

*(As the light becomes brighter and brighter, the sounds of the interstate grow in volume and change pitch becoming deeper and more violent.)*

WILL. Now.

*(The light reaches an uncomfortable level of brightness, and the sound of the interstate becomes increasingly more and more distorted.)*

WILL. Now.

*(As the light reaches it's brightest point, the sounds of the interstate morph into what sounds like one continuous, monotonous explosion—a low, rumbling, unsettling drone that continues throughout the scene.)*

*(ALEX enters, carrying himself differently than before and speaking in a different manner. WILL looks at him.)*

**ALEX.** It never works.

**WILL.** One day.

*(pause)*

**ALEX.** I was up early this morning, went for a drive up to those mountains outside of town. *(pause)* I felt like I should pray. So I got out of the car, and I knelt down on the ground, and I wanted to pray but I couldn't pray anything.

**WILL.** We could pray together before work.

**ALEX.** No, that's not it, I... *(pause)* When I wake up in the morning, I feel sick. I just feel sick most mornings. Like I don't want to get out of bed. And then I see you, and you look so happy. You look perfect.

*(pause)*

**WILL.** I'm not perfect, Danny.

**ALEX.** Yes. You are. I think you're... *(pause)* I see you, and you're so perfect, and I'm—I'm a bad person.

**WILL.** No, you're not.  You're just letting the world get to you. In God's eyes, you're—beautiful. You're perfect.

**ALEX.** Pastor Rick is trying so hard / with me—

**WILL.** One day none of this will matter. When all this is swallowed up. When we become bodies of pure light. Our perfect souls ripped out of these awful bodies and reborn. Both of us. Can you imagine what that will feel like?

*(pause)*

**ALEX.** Will, I'm not sure I believe in God.

*(long silence)*

ALEX. *(cont.)* Say something. *(pause)* Will. Say something.

*(long pause)*

I'm going to walk home tonight.

*(ALEX exits.)*

*(The lights suddenly return to normal, the drone immediately returns to the normal sounds of the interstate.)*

*(WILL stands alone, listening.)*

## END OF PLAY.

## ABOUT THE PLAYWRIGHT

Samuel D. Hunter's recent plays include *A Bright New Boise* (2011 OBIE award for playwriting, 2011 Drama Desk Nomination for Best Play; upcoming production at Woolly Mammoth Theater Company in Fall 2011), *The Whale* (upcoming production at Denver Center in Winter 2012), *Norway* (Phoenix Theatre of Indianapolis; Boise Contemporary Theater), *Jack's Precious Moment* (Page 73 Productions at 59E59), *Five Genocides* (Clubbed Thumb at the Ohio Theater), *I Am Montana* (Arcola Theatre, London; Mortar Theater, Chicago). His newest play, *When You're Here,* was recently workshopped at the Williamstown Theater Festival, and he is a contributing writer to Headlong Theater's *Decade* which will be produced by London's National Theatre in Fall 2011.

He has active commissions from MTC/Sloan, Seattle Rep, South Coast Rep, and Boise Contemporary Theater. His plays have been developed at the O'Neill Playwrights Conference, Bay Area Playwrights Festival, PlayPenn, Ojai Playwrights Conference, the Lark Playwrights Workshop, Juilliard, LAByrinth, Rattlestick, Seven Devils Playwrights Conference, 24Seven Lab and elsewhere.

Internationally, his work has been translated into Spanish and presented in Mexico City and Monterrey, and he has worked in the West Bank with Ashtar Theatre of Ramallah and Ayyam al-Masrah of Hebron. At Ashtar, he co-wrote *The Era of Whales* which was performed in Ramallah and Istanbul.

Awards: 2011 Sky Cooper Prize, 2008-2009 PONY Fellowship from the Lark, two Lincoln Center Le Compte du Nuoy Awards, others. He is a member of Partial Comfort Productions and is an alum of Ars Nova's Playgroup.

He has taught at Fordham University, Rutgers University, Marymount Manhattan College and The University of Iowa. A native of northern Idaho, Sam lives in New York City. He holds degrees in playwriting from NYU, The Iowa Playwrights Workshop and Juilliard.

# OTHER TITLES AVAILABLE FROM SAMUEL FRENCH

## OOHRAH!

### Bekah Brunstetter

*Dramatic Comedy / 4m, 3f / Interior*

Ron is back from his third and final tour in Iraq, and his wife Sara is excited to restart their life together in their new home. When a young marine visits the family, life is turned upside down. Sara's sister is swept off her feet; her daughter Lacey trades her dresses for combat boots, and Ron gets hungry for real military action. In this disarmingly funny and candid drama, Bekah Brunstetter raises challenging questions about what it means when the military is woven into the fabric of a family, and service is far more than just a job.

"The young scribe's talent and potential are obvious in this Southern-basted dramatic comedy about the war mystique as it plays out on the American home front…"
– *Variety*

"…Poignancy and terrific humor in both the writing and performances…"
– *TheatreMania.com*

"If there's anything that stands out about *Oohrah!* at the Atlantic Theater Company's Stage II, it's the off-Broadway introduction of playwright Bekah Brunstetter, whose play is a fascinating, original take on something we've come to see rather often nowadays: the war play…Let's hope we hear her voice uptown again real soon."
– *NYTheatre.com*

# OTHER TITLES AVAILABLE FROM SAMUEL FRENCH

## KINDNESS

## Adam Rapp

*Drama / 2m, 2f / Interior*

An ailing mother and her teenaged son flee Illinois and a crumbling marriage for the relative calm and safety of a midtown Manhattan hotel. Mom holds tickets to a popular musical about love among bohemians. Her son isn't interested, so Mom takes the kindly cabdriver instead, while the boy entertains a visitor from down the hall, an enigmatic, potentially dangerous young woman.

*Kindness* is a play about the possibility for sympathy in a harsh world and the meaning of mercy in the face of devastating circumstances.

"Compelling. A well-crafted mini-thriller, which keeps you in suspense until the final blackout."
– Joe Dziemianowics, *New York Daily News*

"Rapp has raised some provocative questions about the prickly mother/son relationship he has drawn in such detail."
– Marilyn Stasio, *Variety*

"Pungent, vivid...Rapp finds a gentle approach to his characters' physical and emotional pain without turning sentimental. His playful side is on display too." [Four stars]
– Diane Snyder, *Time Out New York*

"Adam Rapp can write dense, tense, funny dialogue."
– Charles Isherwood, *The New York Times*

"A taut and involving dark comedy. Hilarious and unsettling."
– Dan Bacalzo, *TheatreMania.com*

SAMUELFRENCH.COM

# OTHER TITLES AVAILABLE FROM SAMUEL FRENCH

## THE DRUNKEN CITY

### Adam Bock

*Comedy / 3m, 3f / Multiple Sets*

Off on the bar crawl to end all crawls, three twenty-something brides-to-be find their lives going topsy-turvy when one of them begins to question her future after a chance encounter with a recently jilted handsome stranger. *The Drunken City* is a wildly theatrical take on the mystique of marriage and the ever-shifting nature of love and identity in a city that never sleeps.

"A playful and hopeful comedy. Like the best episodes of *Sex and the City,* a little heartache always goes well with hilarity. The cast is appealing, adorable, and top-shelf. There's only one response to something as pleasing as *The Drunken City* - another round!"
– *New York Daily News*

"A lot of fun! Adam Bock's scalpel-sharp insight has made him a potent force on today's theater scene. Trip Cullman pitches the performances at just the right level of wooziness. Tart, smart and intoxicating."
– *The New York Sun*

# OTHER TITLES AVAILABLE FROM SAMUEL FRENCH

## CREATURE

### Heidi Schreck

*Comedy / 3m, 3f / Cimple Set*

After being pestered by devils for more than half a year, Margery Kempe – new mother, mayor's daughter, and proprietress of a highly profitable beer business – is liberated from her torment by a vision of Jesus Christ in purple robes.

Visions are hard to come by, even in 1401. Should we trust the new Margery, with her fasting and her weeping and her chastity fixation, or burn her with the other heretics? Can a woman of insatiable appetites just up and audition for sainthood?

Playwright and OBIE-winning actor Heidi Schreck conjures a collision of contemporary and medieval imaginations: a very funny, a little bit scary new play about faith and its messengers.

"*Creature* indicates that the talented [Heidi Schreck] is a playwright to watch!"
– *New York Post*

"Saints can be hell to live with. That's part of the comedy of *Creature*, Heidi Schreck's absorbing new play about character and faith, loosely based on the life of Margery Kempe, a medieval Englishwoman who, after a difficult childbirth, saw visions of the Devil and Jesus…"
– *The New York Times*